NALAK

ABANINDRANATH TAGORE

NALAK

ABANINDRANATH TAGORE

TRANSLATED FROM BENGALI BY

URBI BHADURI

THORNBIRD

NIYOGI BOOKS

Published by
NIYOGI BOOKS
Block D, Building No. 77,
Okhla Industrial Area, Phase-I,
New Delhi-110 020, INDIA
Tel: 91-11-26816301, 26818960
Email: niyogibooks@gmail.com
Website: www.niyogibooksindia.com

Editor: Mohua Mitra
Design: Shraboni Roy
Illustrations: Nikita Gandhi
Cover illustration: Nikita Gandhi

ISBN: 978-93-89136-09-8
Publication: 2019

Printed at: Niyogi Offset Pvt. Ltd., New Delhi, India

"At this instant, the day ends. The birds clamour one last time. The air is fragrant with the perfume of many flowers, the sky lights up with the radiance of many stars. The full moon rises in the east like a golden umbrella over the sal tree. Precisely at this moment, a baby like a little golden doll is born. Buddhadev is born. Like a second moon is he in this world, covered by yellow champak flowers!"

Abanindranath Tagore

TRANSLATOR'S NOTE

Why this book deserves to be translated:

Though the story of the Buddha is well-known to most of us, *Nalak* is unforgettable because of the sheer lyricism of the storytelling, and the way in which the journey of the Buddha and Nalak are traced parallel throughout. As in unfulfilled love, they never actually cross paths, missing each other by a hairbreadth. But the relationship of the teacher and the disciple is still complete. Nalak realises the Buddha's heart, the heart of his mentor in the lucid darkness of his meditation and himself reaches a state where he floats his own heart out like a flower in a stream, in complete surrender to the teacher.

Nalak is less about the factual events in the Buddha's life; it is more about humanising his actual spiritual journey and the human connections–tiny, beautiful sketches of the unconditional human relationships–that sustain him on his difficult path. It is also a powerful exploration of the terrifying demons of the mind whom Siddharth had to fight in his quest to find the end of all suffering. All of this is brought alive through a series of kaleidoscopic images, resulting in a compelling, almost cinematic telling of the story.

Rishi Debal in meditation while a strange light, like a flower or the rising moon blossoms in the darkness

Rishi Debal was meditating. A little boy called Nalak waited upon him. The forest of *vardhan* trees was dark, the shelter of the banyan tree was dark, darkness lay across the wide river, both banks plunged in dark. It was the dead of night, and the black sky was lit up with stars. The wind was asleep, the water was still, not a leaf stirred in the trees. It was at such a moment when a light blossomed gradually in the darkness—a light like a flower or a rising moon. The earth began to tremble from one side to the other, quite like water droplets quivering and rolling about on a lotus leaf! The Rishi opened his eyes and saw a strange light in the sky. It was not the light of the moon, nor the light of the sun, but a light of all lights fused into one. No one had ever seen such a sight before! It was as if someone had floated a flag of seven colours in the sky, or laid out steps of light through the vacuum for some god to descend. The sannyasi rose from his seat. "Buddhadev is going to take birth in Kapilavastu," he told Nalak. "I am going there to behold him. Take care of yourself in my absence." And he started on the narrow path which wound its way through the forest, travelling northwards.

Nalak sat down to quietly meditate under the banyan tree. Image upon image took shape in front of his eyes.

He saw the king's palace at Kapilavastu. Queen Mayadevi lay asleep on her gold bedstead. The open terrace adjoining her room looked out onto the royal gardens, the town, the temples and the monasteries. Beyond that, far across stood the snowy Himalayas. A wondrous white light beyond them filled up the entire sky, and the sun rose in its centre like a vermilion dot!

King Shuddhodhan was staring at this strange light, when Mayadevi woke up and said, "Maharaj, I had such a beautiful dream! A tiny white elephant, with two tender milk teeth curved like the arcs of the moon on a *dwitiya* night, came down to my lap from over the clouds on the far side of the Himalayas, but again vanished from sight! Oh, and it had this beautiful mark like a vermilion dot on its forehead!"

While the king and queen discussed the dream, morning had dawned. The sounds of the flute floated down from the *nahabatkhana*, the streets resounded with the bustle of pedestrians and the sonorous sounds of conch-shells; and bells rang out from the temple. In the interior chambers of the palace, the queen's maids filled gold tumblers with water for Mayadevi's bath; women garden-tenders arranged flowers for puja on gold plates. The queen's pet peacock wandered in and settled down on the terrace, the pair of lovebirds in their gold cage start quarrelling with the maids for their feed, and a beggar comes to the door with a "Hail the Queen, our Mother!"

As the day progressed, people in the royal palace started discussing the queen's dream.

King Shuddhodhan was seated in the royal court, adorning the throne, as majestic as the sun. He was dressed in scarlet royal robes and a bejewelled crown, an auspicious red-sandalwood mark on his brow. Beside him was the prime minister, and next to him, the bearer of the king's golden sceptre. On the other side of the king stood the umbrella bearer, holding a pure white umbrella over the king's head, and next to him the protector of the polis with his shield and falchion. The courtyards on either side were occupied by Brahmin scholars and by kings and princes from different kingdoms respectively. All around the court stood the king's subjects, surrounded in turn by gatekeepers wearing red turbans and carrying thick sturdy bamboo sticks.

At the centre of the court, directly under the red canopy, eight astrologers sat on eight blood red mattresses, trying to interpret the queen's dream. Holding bits of chalk in their hands, they pored over ancient texts. Some had white hair, some were bald, a few had tied their hair into ponytails while others had straight bristly moustaches. Each of them carried a snail-shell filled with snuff. Some were quilling down their observations; others used chalk to mark out their predictions:

The aspect of the sun in the dream indicates that the royal prince will command sovereign power and might. In the aspect of the moon, he is beautiful to behold, gifted, the King of kings, and will have a long life. The white elephant indicates that his profound and

tranquil nature is rare indeed in this world.
The royal prince is one who will rid humanity of its
sorrow through his reverent mahabuddha *nature.*

"O King, the Shastras never lie. A great man will surely take birth in this Shakya lineage of kings. Rejoice."

Instantly this cry was taken up unanimously everywhere. "Rejoice! Rejoice! Give alms, grain, clothing, lamps, incense and land!"

Joyful music begins to play in the king's palace at Kapilavastu and in the abodes of his subjects. It resounds in the marketplace, in the fields, right up to the river wharfs! The sky smiles, the wind blows stronge out of sheer happiness! The jewel danglers in the king's crown, the pearl fringes in his umbrella, the necklace around the prime minister's neck awarded by the king, the queen's gift of woollen shawls that the scholars have wrapped around themselves, the red cloth of the royal household on the heads of all the servants, the poor, the young and the old—all begin to sway with gaiety and abandon!

The vast unending stretches of garden of the royal household are full of trees – tree after tree – and lush green grass, moist winds, cool shades, birdsong and the fragrance of flowers. In its heart there is a great lotus pond. Beside the pond is a lofty sal tree whose top touches the sky. The marble seat beneath the tree is covered by the flowers that had bloomed amid its branches and leaves, blown down by the south wind.

Evening approaches. The comely women of the neighbourhood come to wash themselves in the lotus pond. They leave. Then a group of garden-tenders come, their hair fastened high on their heads, wearing tight neckpieces and dangling gold earrings. They sweep up the dry leaves and water the flowering trees. Finishing their work in the garden at the close of day, they leave. Nowhere do they leave a speck of dust or a dry twig—not in the green grass, not at the edges of the pond, not underneath the trees.

Night descends now—a full moon night of springtime. The sun dwindles in the west, the moon prepares to rise in the east. On one side of the earth a golden flame, on the other side a sliver of silver! The blue sky overhead, filled with a million stars, rings with the sounds of evening puja and conch shells. At such a moment Mayadevi, along with the women of the royal household, visits the garden in a gold litter lined by silver net. Her female attendants cool her with fans made of flowers. They carry a box filled with fragrant betel-leaf for the Queen.

Mayadevi starts walking in the shades of the trees, hand-in-hand with her most beloved companion. She pauses underneath the towering sal tree in the middle of the garden. She places her left hand on a blossom-filled branch, while her right hand rests on the curve of her waist.

At this instant, the day ends. The birds clamour one last time. The air is fragrant with the perfume of many flowers, the sky lights up with the radiance of many stars. The full moon rises in the east like a golden umbrella over the sal tree. Precisely at this moment, a baby like a little golden doll is born. Buddhadev is born. Like a second moon is he in this world, covered by yellow champak flowers! All places instantly light up—not a single dark corner remains. Buddhadev manifests in Maya mother's lap, cooling the breast of mother earth. He is like a single dewdrop on a lotus leaf—pure, exquisite, and tiny!

Very soon the Lumbini gardens fill with people. King Shuddodhan comes to see his son, along with all his

Nalak in deep meditation, experiences the vision of the birth of Buddhadev

courtiers and friends. The attendants begin to blow on the conch-shell, and make the auspicious *ulu* sound with their tongues and pursed up lips. The heavens rain flowers, the trumpet of the gods sound from amid the clouds, conch-shells blow from every earthly abode, and the underworld resounds with the sonorous, celebratory sounds of drums. Buddhadev, born amidst the tumultuous rejoicing of the three worlds, takes his first seven steps upon the earth. Wherever his beautiful feet touch the ground, there springs up, penetrating the depths of the three underworlds, *atal*, *sutal*, and *rasatal*, a gold lotus like a spinning wheel made of fire. Seven clouds from the heavens immediately bring forth the water of seven seas, and begin to water it.

Nalak watches in amazement as the gods, demons and humans come together to ceremoniously initiate Buddhadev into kingship in the midst of the seven lotuses. Suddenly his mother comes calling—"You daredevil boy! The Rishi's not here and here you are sitting all alone in the forest! No time for sleep, meals, or lessons! All you want is to close your eyes and meditate…at this age this boy has already become a *sannyasi*! Come, come back home!"

Mother pulls Nalak by his hands; Nalak rolls on the ground crying—"Let me go, Ma, one more time! Let me see what happens next! I beg you, Ma, let go, let go!" The whole forest cries with Nalak—"Let go…let go!" In vain, for Nalak has been taken back home and put under lock and key.

They have forcefully sent Nalak to the Guru's primary school.

The Guru says—"*Okash ahang bhantey*!"

Nalak reads—"*Bhantey*".

The Guru says—"Write, *Anug gahang katta shilang detha mey bhantey!*"

Nalak writes in big letters on the palm-leaf, "*Shilang detha mey bhantey.*" His mind is neither in the writing, nor in the reading. His being is in the *vardhan* forest in the shade of the banyan tree and in the capital of Kapilavastu.

◀ *Nalak in school, watching the* kubo *bird from the window*

From the window of the straw-thatched schoolroom, a *tintiri* tree can be seen—some *kaash* and a growth of thorn, a thicket of bamboo and a pond. A little slice of the afternoon sun has fallen there. A red crested *kubo* bird alights on the branch with a rustle, and begins its "*kub kub*" cry. A black bee hums over the flowers of the thorn tree. It hovers near the window and again flies away. Nalak looks at it wistfully, thinking—Oh, if only I had wings like them, could Ma ever shut me up in a room? I would have run to the forest in a single sprint.... And the Guru's voice breaks through his reverie, "Continue writing, boys." At once the bird of the woods flies away, and the scratching sound of the quills on the palm leaves resumes. Only Nalak knows what agony he is in! His hand refuses to move, yet he must not cease writing. He feels like crying but still he has to continue reading the alphabets–"*Jo ro lo, so, sho, shho*"–be it cloudy or hot, morning or afternoon!

When Nalak returns home from school holding his mother's hand, sometimes the east wind blows, stirring the crowns of the palm trees that stand tall above the sal. Crows caw fearfully in the bamboo thicket. Nalak longs for a storm to come, to demolish and sweep away the whole village in its wake, the entire village along with its school roof thatched with straw. Then they would be forced to live in the forest and there would be no means of confining him again! In the night the wind blows gustily outside their room. Whenever there is a spark of lightning, Nalak begins to pray fervently... Come Storm, Come Rain! Let the earthen walls be washed away, let the stronghold of the door break down!

«««»»

Storm comes, so does rain. Everything gets submerged under water. But alas! The door doesn't open; the walls do not fall apart. Confinement persists. Oh for the open fields! Oh for the *vardhan* forest encircled by the wide open vault of sky! How will Nalak ever return to you! The place where birds fly happily, the deer play freely and joyfully, the place under the trees where the wind blows freely, and no one can hold you back, where you can play around and fly with abandon!

Nalak is intensely hoping and counting the days for the return of the Rishi. In the meanwhile Debal Rishi is returning from Kapilavastu, with the sacred dust from Buddha's feet smeared all over his body. He is dancing his way back with both hands joyfully lifted up, singing through the villages—

"Namo namo Buddhadivakaraya.
Namo namo Gautam chandrimaya.
Namo anantagunarnabaya, namo
Shakyanandanaya."

It is the autumnal season of Sarat. The sky is golden; the fields on both sides of the path are filled with golden grain. It is a time when no one wants to stay cooped up at home anymore! Kings leave with their entourage of horses to conquer kingdoms, people come out of home and make their way to the market, the fields or the wharf. Some carry wares on their heads, some go out to reap the paddy in the fields, others go out on business in lands beyond the seven seas and thirteen rivers. And the people who have no other work start walking in the Rishi's wake, singing his song —"*Namo namo Buddhadivakaraya!*"

It is evening. There is not a single trace of cloud in the blue sky. Moonlight streams

◀ ***Debal Rishi and Nalak walk towards the forest while Nalak's mother weeps***

down from the sky to the earth; the Milky Way is visible overhead like a lighted strip of net across from north to south. As he travels along the village paths, Debal Rishi sings—"*Namo namo Gautamchandrimaya.*" The little boy in his mother's lap listens to—"*Namo namo Gautamchandrimaya!*" The mother sitting at the edge of the yard hears—"*Namo namo*"; the old grandmother from inside the room hears—"*Namo.*" Instantly she tells everybody—"Say *nomo*, quickly!" The conch shells and bells from the zamindar's house ring in the same tune along with the Rishi's song—*Namo namo namo!* Finally, when the night draws to an end, the lotus, weighed down by overnight dew says "*Namo*", the moon slants to the west, saying "*Namo*", it was then that Nalak wakes up from sleep, sits up and sees the Rishi in front of his eyes! The door is open. Golden sunlight streams in and reaches across to fall directly on his head. Nalak rises and touches the Rishi's feet. The Rishi blesses Nalak—"Be happy, be free."

Nalak comes out on the road holding the hand of his mentor. His mother wipes her tears with the edge of her sari. "Please do not take Nalak away," she tearfully implores the Rishi. "I do not have anybody else in this world."

The Rishi replies—"Don't be sad. You will get your son back after thirty-five years. Come, fearlessly surrender him to the feet of the Buddha."

The Rishi begins to chant and Nalak's mother, holding both her son's hands in her own, repeats after him—

"*Kushumang phullitang etang paggahettwan anjaling*
Buddha sheshthang sabittwan aakashemapipujaye."
(I worship the Buddha under the pure sky;
I worship the Buddha with my beautiful [Nalak] flower.)

And the Rishi goes away towards the forest, holding Nalak's hand.

«««»»

Once again, the old *vardhan* forest, the shade of the banyan tree. Debal Rishi and a group of holy men are sitting around a fire. The tridents in their hands catch the light of the fire and glitter. Deep in the interiors of the forest, nothing is visible in the *kohl*-like darkness except the bright sunlight glinting like heated gold on the clusters of *ashwattha* leaves, on the sturdy tree roots and on the knotted hair of the sannyasis, like the spark of lightning on a cloud!

Nalak is quietly meditating, enveloped by the silent darkness of the forest, and the deep blue sky overhead. Not a breath, not a whisper sounds anywhere. No one speaks a word. Only, from time to time, Debal Rishi's question—"Then what?"

Pictures form before Nalak's eyes and he renders them in words: "King Shuddhodhan is sitting on his ivory throne covered by deer-skin, holding Buddhadev in his lap. On either side of him are four astrologers. Right in front of him there is the sacred fire of *hom puja*. On the other side, amidst heaps of unripe paddy grains, *durba* grass, conch-shells, bells, flowers, sandalwood and incense, is Mother Gautami. The puja is over. The King asks the Brahmins—'What is the name suitable for the prince?'

"The Brahmins say—'The people of this world will derive all prosperity and fulfilment from the Prince; hence his name is Siddharth. If the Prince becomes the king, he will gain all the wealth in the world. If he doesn't become king, he will redeem the world by attaining Buddhatwa. He will liberate His Self by attaining nirvana after death. Hence he is called Siddharth.'

"The King asks—'Please determine whether Kumar Siddharth will become king and rule, or whether he will leave everything and go to the forests to strive for Buddhatwa?'

"The eight astrologers begin to chalk out their calculations. The first of them, Sriram Acharya, lifts up two fingers to the King—'O Maharaj, he can be a king, or be a holy man. It is difficult to say, the pull is equal on both sides.'

"Ram's brother Lakshman immediately closes both eyes and says—'I agree with my brother.'

"Jayadhwaj twists both hands and says—'Yes, and No.'

"Srimontin inclines his neck on both sides and says—'Those are my very words.'

"Bhoj opens his eyes wide and says—'I can see this, as well as that.'

"Sudatta moves his neck to the right, then to the left, and reports—'I see this direction, as well as that.'

"Sudatta's brother Sudam draws snuff into both nostrils and says—'I can also see the same thing that my brother has predicted.'

"Only Koundinyo, younger than all of them yet wiser than any, holds up a single finger towards the King.

'Maharaj, it is not this direction or that, either This or That,' he says. 'It is beyond question that the prince will go in no other direction except that of the Buddha. He will not remain at home. The day he sees a desolate old man ravaged by age, a poor man pitifully invaded by disease, a dead man and a beggar hermit, that day Kumar Siddharth will go away, leaving your resplendent home in darkness, just as a bird gnaws through its gold chain and flies away.'

The holy men in the forest stand up with a solemn roar. Nalak opens his eyes. It is morning.

«««»»

From that day onward, Nalak is not able to see anything anymore. He meditates, but all that he sees is a great and terrifying wall made of gold bricks. It blazes like fire in the light of the sun; it shuts out the blue of the sky and the free motions of the air. It has neither an end, nor a visible beginning. The bird of Nalak's mind soars, but returns empty-handed every time, obstructed by the wall.

Days pass by, months go by like this. Whole years pass. On one side of the golden wall is Siddharth; on the other side, Nalak. They are just like the bird inside the cage and the bird of the forest.

Fearing that his son might leave home to become a holy man, King Shuddhodhan imprisoned Siddharth amid golden dreams, laughter and flute music, festivities and merrymaking, quite like a bird in a golden cage. On summer days the heat of the sun begins to rise, water dries up, the hot air begins to burn. In the monsoons new clouds appear, the earth is swept away by the flow of running water and the currents of the rivers become faster. In the autumnal season of Sarat the sky takes on a blue hue, white clouds fly riding the thin air, river water shifts and sandy shores are revealed. In winter the landscape is covered by snow and mist, leaves fall and flowers languish. Again in Basanta (spring) the whole world is filled with flowers and fruit, fragrance fills the sky and joy bursts forth in the blowing of the south winds, in moonlight and birdsong.

But whatever the season, in his royal temple surrounded by the golden wall, Buddhadev feels just what the caged bird feels. He wants to break free of his golden confines

Siddhartha and Nalak separated by the golden wall, like the caged bird and the free bird in the forest

and emerge into the world. At times he seems to hear the whole world crying to him. On summer days and on stormy nights, in the Sarat evenings, on wintry mornings and in the passing hours of spring, the world cries out to him. It calls out to him through the "kuhu!" call of the cuckoo bird, through the sounds of the blowing gusts of wind, through the patter of falling rain, through the shivers of winter, and through the murmurs of the leaves. It seems to implore him with tears—"Come out, come out! Save us, salvage us! The fire of suffering is blazing in the three worlds, the fire of death is raging, life is shrivelling up in sorrow and intense pain! See how our tears sweep us away, how the overwhelming tides of suffering collapse the embankments of the mind! Joy is but the instant's flash of lightning in the sky—gone in a blink! Happiness is like the clouds of Sarat that linger not, but float away! Life is like the white *shiuli* flower that languishes with the winter's dew! The gay season of spring does not last forever. Alas, who will put out the fire of sorrow, the pyre of death that burns day and night in this world? Who else – but you – can drive out Fear from this world? Do not live in oblivion in the world of maya. Tear apart the noose of flowers – come out – set us free! Come out and give refuge to the world of living creatures."

The soul of Nalak, the souls of the people of the world, the soul of the sky and that of the air thirst to set eyes on Buddhadev. Their longing sometimes falls on the earth as rain, sometimes it storms down and throws itself against the golden wall. Sometimes it becomes Light, and calls, "Come!" It becomes Darkness and implores, "Save us!" It blossoms as a bright flower, and again sheds off like a dry leaf. The laughter and tears, the life and the death of the universe daily transpire in front of Siddharth's eyes, through days and nights, spanning months and years, in many ways and in many directions.

One day Siddharth sees a row of geese flying across the blue sky like a garland of *parijat* flowers. How joyous they are! Thousands of wings rise and fall together in the same rhythm, and they sound the same strain together, on, on, on and on! The sky responds to this cry; white-sailed clouds sail along with them. The wind journeys with them as well, pushing cloud after cloud. The earth answers their cry in the journey of the river towards the ocean, and the movement of the ocean towards the river, breaking mountains and pushing sands on its way.

In the midst of so much joyful movement and utterance, an arrow from an unseen hand pierces the wing of one of the geese like a bolt of lightning. Instantly all corners of the earth shudder with a cry of pain. The bird pierced by the arrow drops down at Siddharth's feet like a flower from a ripped garland, drops of blood spattering across its body.

Oh, where does all that joy go? The ride on the air, the song in the blue sky? In one instant all happiness, all the life energy of the world is spent. The sky is empty; the wind's motion stops. A single arrow causes all talk, all movement, all play to cease.

The sounds of distant heartbreaking lament and weeping begin to ring in Siddharth's ears and his heart. Day and night, in every arrival, departure and in every movement, in the midst of happiness and peace, in every work he undertakes, in pleasure and in festivity, he hears the sound of wailing. It seems to him that laments have filled the entire universe, the lament of the smallest of the small, the lament of the oldest of the old.

«««»»

After days and nights of continuous storm and rain, finally darkness has dispersed today. The cloud curtain

Siddharth at the castle and the wounded bird at his feet

has shifted to let the morning light filter through from the east. The sky smiles happily, the breeze blows gaily. The clouds are tinged by honey-coloured light. The birds in the forests, the farmers in the villages, and the children in their homes sing Madhumangal songs today. Siddharth looks out from the eastern doorway. There seems to be no sorrow in the world today, no tears! As far as he can see, as much as he can hear, it is joy, and only joy! Happiness is in the green of the fields. Happiness has bloomed in flowers in the woods and glens. In each and every home young boys and girls, decked up in new clothes, smile in glee. They play with new toys that shine and jingle with rapture. Happiness rains showers of flowers from every leaf and creeper. Joy blows in gold dust along the roads, like the colourful *abir* of Holi.

Today in the lap of all this jubilation, Siddharth's golden chariot travels slowly towards the east, towards the morning light and in the direction of the end of darkness. There is no sorrow in the world today, no grief, no tears. There is only joy—the joy of awakening after sleep, the joy of light after darkness, joy like blooming flowers and swinging garlands, the joy of waking up to the sounds of singing and flute music. Nothing is perishing nor languishing in the world today.

At such a moment, from an unknown quarter, a figure comes and stands in front of Siddharth's chariot. It blots out all the light and joy of the morning, just as a flame is snuffed off in a storm. It is an old man, toothless, eternal and endless, leaning on his stick! There is no flesh on his body, only a few bones. He is bent over with age, with shaking limbs and trembling neck! When he talks, his voice also shakes. He can see nothing nor hear anything. He walks slowly from the light into the darkness, his hands held out in front of him like two charred bones, absolutely alone in the world. He has no strength, no means, not a single being to call his own. No son nor daughter, no friend or well-wisher. All his kin have fallen and perished. All the vital juices of his life have dried up. All drama of existence, all play is over. Light now hurts his eyes, all music is tuneless, all forms of joy are grief to him! Enveloping himself in his darkness, his hurt, his grief and his burning suffering like a torn tattered blanket, he is walking away from joy and light. He has become such that life itself runs away from him, music falls silent in his presence, and joy does not dare to come within paces of him. The sight of him makes beauty perish out of fear! Casting a black shadow over morning light, smiling its chilling toothless smile, this awful demonic figure obstructs Siddharth's way, and says—"Look at me. I am the Decay of old age. I spare none, I wither everything, perish everything, suck up, loot everything! Remember me Prince! You too will be mine one day—your blue blood shall not save you!" And the figure surveys all, laughing a terrifying laugh.

Instantly, all the light of the sky and the green of the fields are blotted out under his gaze. The fields burn, rivers dry up. All that is fresh and new becomes old and stale. Siddharth sees mountains come crashing down, trees uprooted, everything reduced to dust. And in the midst of all this he sees the figure, its white hair tossed by the wind, dragging its torn blanket along the dust slowly, one step at a time – the eternal endless toothless terrible figure of Withering – extinguishing light, quenching joy, sucking, looting everything, walking away, alone, playing on cymbals made of bones.

«««»»

It is another day. Siddharth's golden chariot is emerging from the southern gateway of Kapilavastu, its banner billowing in the gentle breeze with its scent of many flowers, and its cool sandalwood touch on the skin soothes all heat and fever. It is the sweet southern wind that causes flowers to bloom and soothes the soul. The cowherds' flutes can be heard from distant meadows. The *kuhu* melody of *papia* birds come floating across from far-off forests.

People have opened their doors wide and emerged out of their homes today. There is singing under the stars, amidst the open winds. A cool blue glow lights up the sky, and there is a cool play of light and shadow all over the earth. The light, liberating wind blows from the south across the water and on land, and across the woods and glens, at home and in the outdoors. It brings a tangible touch of happiness, it plays the flute of joy. It sways the heart with joy and fills up the mind's sails. The chariot of Siddharth's mind floats and dances along with it, to the rhythm of the lovebird's tune, along the still waters of the ocean of bliss. The *suktara* constellation gazes down at the earth, like a flower blooming in a dream world! The light of happiness is showering down, the wind of happiness is blowing gently in all the four directions. It seems that for today at least, all maladies, all unhappiness have fled far away. Today there is no irritability anywhere. Today, for once, everything and everybody in the whole wide world is happy and contented.

Suddenly, drawing aside the blissful curtain of dreams, a jaundiced figure floats up in front of Siddharth's eyes. He is fever-ravaged, pitifully ill. Unable to stand, he reels; unable to walk, he is down in the dust and the mud. Sometimes he shivers with cold, at other times he cries out for water to soothe the pain of his burning body! All the blood in his body seems to be concentrated in and pouring forth from his bloodshot eyes. That look in his eyes has made the whole sky fiery, livid. All his living blood seems to have turned to water, flowing down his paper-pale, deathly-chill body. On touching him, the wind turns icy. With every breath in, he seems to want to suck away the life of the whole world. With every breath out, he seems to be spreading his burning pain in the entire existence of life.

Siddharth watches as all the light of earthly existence extinguishes right in front of his eyes. The wind dies down; all speech and song fall silent. The only audible sound comes from the heart of that dirt and mud-covered pale figure. It is like someone hammering on

Siddharth witnesses Old Age, Sickness (Fever), and Death

a stone wall—*dhhak, dhhak*. In tandem with that beat, the stars of the sky are blown out, and lit up again; the wind keeps blowing.

Having looked upon the terrible face of Fever, Siddharth returns home, to the midst of royal luxury, to the bank of the sea of pleasure. But he continues to hear that heartbeat inside his chest, beating against his ribs.

«««»»

This time the gold chariot moves through the western gateway, in the direction of the setting sun and of the end of day. People avert their faces from this direction as they return home. The birds return chirping to their nests in the branches of trees, to their leafy retreats. Cows and their calves walk back along the edges of the meadows and the riverbanks to their sheds, their bodies covered by the gold dust of late afternoon. Shepherd children playing on their flutes walk back along the village roads to their earthen homes, back to the laps of their mothers. People are on their way home after the day's buying and selling in distant markets. Everyone returns home, those who were far away and those who were close by. The lamp of the sky holds out light for those who are homeless; the lamp of Durga ma burning under the tulsi sapling in the courtyard lights the way back for those who were at work, at lessons, or at play. People look at these two lights, as still and unwavering as a mother's gaze, as they return home today, to their mothers' laps, to their brothers and sisters, to the company of friends. Even the beggar happily strums an *agamani* tune to welcome Ma Durga home on his *ektara* and sings along, "Oh mother of mine, the mother has come home, the mother…". The sounds of conch shells celebrating reunions can be heard from every household. The tune of *agamani*, the tune of homecoming, the tune of falling with abandon into the arms of loved ones, the tune of sitting on a loved one's lap and putting arms around the necks—this is the tune playing in the breeze today, peeping inside open doors, and calling out in empty rooms. Empty lives and hearts brim with this music today, the music of regaining something lost, the music of holding loved ones close to one's heart, the music of finally finding the lost ones!

Today Siddharth can see no dearth of joy, not even a little gap through which sorrow may filter. The bliss all around, complete like a full river, like a full moon, has lit up the whole of existence, and plunged it in life-giving waters. The river of happiness is in high tide. Nothing is dry, nothing forlorn or empty today.

Wherever he looks, Siddharth finds the joys of reunion everywhere on his travels on this day. He sees happiness moving in droves and clusters, forcefully pushing doors open, falling into each other's arms, and lovingly embracing necks. Nobody is forgotten today. No one is separate, no one is going away or letting go. Is there anyone who is not joyful today? Is there any place devoid of joy? Is there anyone who is feeling sad today? Who can be shedding tears? Who can be sad, today of all days?

As if in answer to his questions, the bell of some derelict temple registers three mighty tolls. Pain exists, pain exists, pain still exists—it seems to say. All at once the sleeping world is roused by a rude jolt and the strains of heartbreaking sobbing ring out—alas alas alas! A sobbing that tugs painfully at the thirty-two veins of the breast, threatening to burst the sky open, and slice through the wind!

Siddharth is roused suddenly from his blissful dream. He looks at the sky, but the light of the stars has turned murky like the eyes of dead men. Halfway between the second and third watches of the night, he sees a net of pale yellow over land and water, as if somebody is slowly drawing a white sheet to cover the dead face of the earth. The lamps burning in houses start guttering between burning and extinction, extinction and burning, then go out all of a sudden and burn no more. No light remains anywhere. No answer emerges from anywhere, nothing makes a sound anymore. Half of the sky is filled with a moisture-laden black cloud that droops like a pair of tearful, wet eyelashes. It sheds a drop or two of rain, like tears. Amidst all this, Buddhadev sees congregations of people walking past. They are carrying thousands of dead bodies wrapped up in white sheets on their shoulders, in their laps, across their chests. Their feet touch the earth, yet make no noise. Their breasts swell with uncontainable grief, yet no word escapes their lips. They walk rapidly and mechanically with their sorrowful eyes fixed towards the riverbank, where light is fading in the wake of the setting sun, where the day is ending. They walk towards the banks of the river where bodies are cremated, away, far far away from home, far away from the refuge of arms and laps, away from any prospect of ever returning home, of ever being enfolded in arms, of being gathered up in laps. It is the path of going away in tears, leaving behind loved ones, falling behind on the way.

The lament of death and the fire of cremation are on either side. Through their midst leads the path of leaving forever in tears, leaving behind those one loves. From time to time, a gust of wind like a hot breath blows quantities of ash on the faces and into the eyes of the travellers on that death-path. The ash makes their hair white, their skin deathly pale! Ash flies about, hot from the burning and charring of all substance. The ash of a dead fire fly around, so do the ashes of life, and even death. Happiness, grief, indeed all aspects of existence turn to ash and blow away, far far away, like a pale grey strip of cloud through the open sky overhead. Buddhadev sees a mother holding up the dead body of her son and staring at him unblinkingly. The wind laments as it moves around—alas, alas! When he returns home that day, in place of the blooming lotus in his gold flowerpot, Siddharth finds a fistful of ash, and a charred bone from the breast of a dead man.

«««»»

It is another day. The freezing wind slices through the bosom like a knife. Wintry fog has permeated, covering all directions. Sunlight does not reach the earth, nor starlight—day and night appear the same. In the diffused light, all colours seem to be hues of black and white, all things seem to be at a great distance, so covered in mist are they, so much wiped over by dewy moisture. Siddharth stands at a window open to the north. All greenery, all flowers and leaves are covered over by snow and mist; the frozen pressure of ice had made the large and the small, the ups and the downs of roads level. Not a single bird flies or sings its way through the sky today. The wind does not carry the scent of a single flower, nor the smallest touch of happiness. Not a single strain of joy comes floating through! It is as if the white snow, chilling mists and silent winter have made everything soundless, unmoving and stone-like, as if the earth herself has lost consciousness.

Standing amidst the chill-laden mists of the north and the white snow, Siddharth wonders for days on end—will light never draw aside these misty nets and show itself? Will joy never appear, melting the ice, blooming the flowers and filling the earth with colour and beauty?

There is an unanswering hush everywhere. Siddharth listens carefully but there is no sound, no answer forthcoming from any direction. It is a world neither lighted nor dark, an in-between place neither night nor day can call its own.

Siddharth stood wrapped in profound silence. As far as he could see there were walls of ice and curtains of fog. Peeping through is the Decay of Old Age, with his hoary head. There is Fever, shivering with a pale bloodless face, staring at emptiness. Death is also visible, wrapped in an icy white sheet. Siddharth could see himself and every soul ever created reflected on the dense curtain of fog and on the frozen walls of ice, as clearly as seeing his own reflection in a mirror, or seeing pictures on a white piece of paper. He could see the birth of every creature, it reaching senility and decrepitude, and then perishing. Great Fear with his bloodied trident chased all of them. Fever, Decay and Death ran along in his heels like three hunter dogs, splitting open, tearing things apart with their teeth and nails! Nothing is able to withstand them, nothing escapes them. When they jump into the river, it dries up in fear. When they hurl themselves upon the mountain, it is ground to dust. They wrench children from their mothers' laps, they break down doors and tear up roots. Kings and their subjects, the big and the small alike, fly from Fear, and are blown along like dead leaves over the dust. Everything trembles and droops in great fear; everything dies, and is extinguished like candles in the wind before an approaching storm. Nothing can sit still for a moment. Fear roars its lament as it travels across the sky; blowing across on the wind, it bellows its invitation to die; it is on the prowl in water and on land, inside homes as well as outdoors. It is the Fear of Fever, Decay and Death! Whither happiness? Whither peace? Whither rest? Siddharth could see Fear inside his mind and in front of his eyes. Fear roared like a thunderbolt on top of his head. It had seized the ground under his feet and shook up the foundations of the earth. It had thrown its gigantic net and trapped everything from all directions. The whole world inside the trap begged and implored in vain. Thousands of terrified hands tried to clutch the sky, the air is filled with cries of, "Save us! Salvage us!"

But who can save? Who can salvage? The trap of Fear is on all sides! Is there anybody who is fearless, anybody who does not have any sorrow, any grief? A being so powerful that he can rip apart the unbreakable web of Maya (illusion) and rescue the world from the clutches of Fear?

As if in answer to Siddharth's question, a cry resonates in the sky and wind, in water and land, in the east and the west, north and south–*Biddha Mohiddhhika*–The Mighty Buddhas!

> *Shadebakashsha lokashsha shabbe ete parayana.*
> *Deepa, natha pathishtha, ch tana lena ch paninang.*
> *Gati, bandhu, mahashshasha, sharana ch hiteshino.*
> *Mahappabha, mahateja, mahapancha, mahabbala.*
> *Maha karunika dheera shabbeshanang sukhabaha.*

They are the Buddhas who guide the people of the three worlds on The Path. They are the greatly radiant, possessing sovereign might, the tremendously wise ones. Emanating great power, tranquility and compassion, they bring happiness to all. These greatest of Well-Wishers pray for the good of existence and offer refuge to people who have been washed away by the tides of earthly existence. They are the bank where no land is visible, protectors of the orphaned, shelters for the buffeted, the Path for those who have lost their way,

Friends of those who have nobody to call their own, the Hope for people who have lost faith. They are the Saviours of the world.

And gradually the all-encompassing vision of Fear fades away from Siddharth's eyes and mind, in the way darkness is dispelled before light. He watches as the fog of the skies now starts raining on the earth as light. This light melts the snow and covers the earth in green hues, flowers and leaves. Joy reawakens. This light is in the song of birds in the forests and glens, and in the flute music of the outside world. Internally it overflows as happiness and peace. In all the three worlds of Heaven, Earth and the Underworld, this light lays open the path of happiness, and blows the seven-coloured flag of peace.

Siddharth sees someone walking along this path—it is Himself! He is barefoot, his head uncovered. He has no Fear, no Sorrow, no Grief. He is the Ever-joyous One, walking blissfully over ice and through mists. He offers refuge to everyone and distributes happiness. Fear is trembling near his feet like a little shadow! The web of illusion has been torn apart under his feet, like scattered strips of cloud!

Siddhartha at the castle, seeing himself as monk

As on all the other days, that day also Siddharth directs his chariot back and returns home. But his heart is no longer in the royal temple protected and insulated by the web of illusion, gilded over with golden dreams! His dispassionate soul left those rooms and wandered away, travelling along the banks of unnamed rivers, and through so many unknown lands—alone, unafraid.

«««»»

Siddharth's wife Yashodhara is the new mother of a baby boy. The boy's innocent young face resembles the tender flowers that bloom with the rising of the evening star. But neither Yashodhara's sweet smile nor her beautiful face, neither the joyful songs of her female companions, nor the seven-coloured garlands of light in the homes of Kapilavastu could draw Siddharth's mind back towards a homebound existence any more. He could not remain at home any longer.

Thinking that as Siddharth had become a father, now he would finally settle down to home and hearth, King Shuddhodhan named the new boy Rahul. But how could Siddharth's heart remain at home any longer? Rahul remained, Rahul's mother remained, Siddharth's home, friends and loved ones remained. King Shuddhodhan remained as well, holding on to all of these. Siddharth alone went away to follow the direction of his heart.

«««»»

It is a full moon night in the month of Asharh. Everybody is asleep in the royal household. In the dead of night, Siddharth extinguished the lights and stopped the music. He called, "Chhandak, bring me my horse." Siddharth's attendant Chhandak, who had pledged his life to serving at Siddharth's feet, dressed up the horse Kanthak in a gold harness and brought him to the palace. Siddharth rode his horse to the banks of the river Anoma. The palace of Kapilavastu vanished in the darkness behind him. In front of him was a path filled with the light of the full moon!

Then Chhandak went back to Kapilavastu with the prince's crown, his bracelets, his necklace, his earrings and his horse. Siddharth crossed the river, and walked away towards the forest, to begin on his deep search that would reveal the end of sorrow.

It was a small river, small to look at, and its name was also befittingly, Noma; some call it Anaama (that which

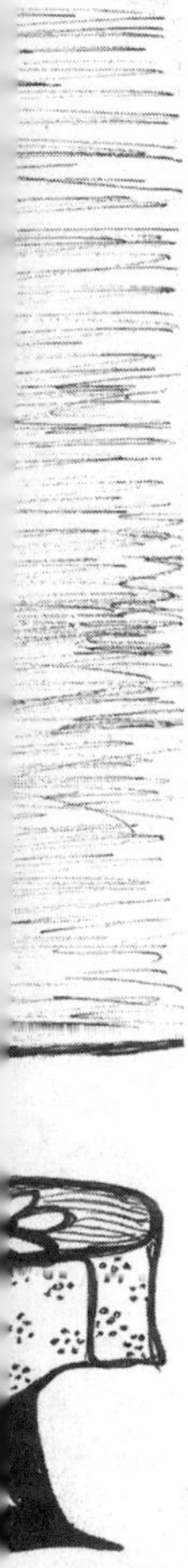

is unnamed), some call it Anoma, some Anama. The bank from which Siddharth had crossed over was ground that was continuously being eroded, without a proper wharf, filled with only rocks and thorns. However, the side where Siddharth alighted, the wharf had sloped down directly to the water's edge; the road lay in the shade of many trees. The path through the forest was full of green grass and made beautiful by wildflowers. Between these two banks was the water of the Noma river, washing the sands, flowing over them at its own leisurely pace. A fisherman was catching fish with a little net. Siddharth gave him his golden shawl and walked away, covering himself with the latter's torn rags.

The river wanders on its way along mango and jackfruit forests, its water lapping the foot of the little hills, sometimes headed eastwards, sometimes south. Siddharth walks in the shade of trees, happily following its course. This place makes one feel like settling down to stay here forever, in its green shades and moist winds.

◀ *Siddharth leaving the royal palace in the dead of night, while Yashodhara and Rahul continue to sleep*

Siddharth spends seven days and seven nights in an ashram of hermits that is housed beneath a leaf-covered, fruit-filled *jaam* tree bent low over the river. After that he reaches the township of Vaishali. The great scholar Arhar Kalam, with his knotted hair, has his den in the outskirts of the town. He has three hundred followers there. Under his guidance, Siddharth read the Shastras, learnt meditation, *asanas*, yoga, tantra and mantras, but did not learn how to conquer sorrow. He again set out on his way.

Surrounded by the Vindhya hills is the town of Rajgeha. It is ruled by the king of Magadh, Bimbisar. Siddharth took shelter beside the town inside a cave of the Ratnagiri hills.

Dawn was about to break when Siddharth descended from the hills and stood on the streets of the township, saying, "Give me alms". The drowsy town just woken up opened its sleepy eyes and saw the young hermit. With so much beauty, a smile wrapped in such compassion, a golden body built up of so much joy, his two eyes full of such tranquility, reassuring with one hand, begging with the other hand, purifying the town streets with the dust of his feet—the town had seen nobody like him before!

Those who were walking away turned back to look at him. Leaving their play, young boys gathered near him. Women removed the edge of the sari covering their heads and gazed at him. Nobody seemed to feel any fear or shame in looking at him.

King Bimbisar came down to the street to look at him. So many hermits came to beg for alms, but nobody like him ever before! The main street of the town was filled with people who had gathered to catch a glimpse and to place alms in his palm. Shopkeepers felt like looting their shops whole and offering it to him, warekeepers wanted to empty out their wares and give it to him! Even the beggar emptied out his bag of alms and said—"Accept these alms, please!" Siddharth's hands were full of alms yet people's hearts still overflowed with the desire to give! They heaped pearls upon gems, gold and silver, flowers, fruits, rice and pulses at Siddharth's feet. They would not take no for an answer.

Accepting alms that day at every door, Siddharth satisfied the yearnings of the ruler and the ruled, of the great and the small in an unprecedented way. Never again would the world give alms in this way again, nor would alms ever be received in such a way ever. The quantity of gems and pearls, gold and silver, clothes and jewellery that had overflowed and scattered over the roads of Rajgeha amounted to treasure that no king even had ever seen before! Siddharth kept only a fistful of dry rice for himself and, distributing the rest of that peerless treasure to the poor people of Magadh, started on his way again.

«««»»

Udarak Pundit had opened a centre of learning in the neighbourhood of Goyali with seven hundred followers. Siddharth started learning the Shastras from the scholars there. At the time, there was no one to match Udarak's scholarship in entire India. People used to say that the head of Vyasdev and the abdomen of Ganesh had combined to produce the deity reborn called Udarak Shastri.

In a very short time, Siddharth became an unmatched scholar in all the Shastras. No dharma, no way of religion or Shastra remained unknown to him. Finally one day he asked his teacher, "How is sorrow banished?"

Udarak told Siddharth, "Come, let us – you and I – open a large centre of learning and send out news in all directions. Students will come to us from all countries, and then we can spend our days in happiness and freedom from worry. This stomach is the root of all sorrow. Keep it happy, and suffering will not venture within paces of you."

Siddharth saluted Udarak Shastri from a distance and took his leave. He saw Udarak's seven hundred followers carrying loads of sweetmeats along the village roads, to ensure the contentment of their teacher's hunger pangs.

Siddharth left the village path and began to walk through the forest. Inside the forest, he met Koundinyo. It was Koundinyo who had predicted in the King's court that Siddharth would surely leave home and attain 'Buddhatwa'. There were four other Brahmin boys with Koundinyo. They had all become hermits and had left Kapilavastu in order to become Siddharth's disciples.

Beside the river Anjana are the Urayil forests. Siddharth started to meditate there, with the aim of realising the end of sorrow. He meditated there for years on end, according to what the Shastras had prescribed and the directives of teachers.

The meditation was difficult, rigid and very intense. Nobody had ever done it this way before—all through winter, summer, rains and storms, holding the same yogic posture, going without food! The rigid observance made his body dry as wood, draining it of every single drop of blood. Looking at him, nobody could say whether he was even alive anymore!

Siddharth had so much strength, beauty, joy and so much fire in him. Each of these perished one by one during the course of this terrible period of austerity. He was not recognisable as a human being any more, and looked more like a withered tree standing up!

A long time passed like this. It was now the beginning of a new year, the month of Baisakh. There are new leaves, new fruits and flowers on the trees. All the birds, butterflies, deer and peacocks in the forest of Urayil have awakened to some unknown

Siddharth at the Urayil forest, meditating under the banyan tree ▶

joy. They run about, fly, sing and play. The five disciples of Siddharth hear someone strumming on the *ektara* and singing very deep inside the forest. After a long time, they spot Siddharth's still eyelids quivering a little—like dry petals stirred by the wind. The day was drawing to an end. The vermilion light of the end of day filtered through the trees and lay stretched out on the ground, extending from the river bank up to the forest path, like a saffron robe.

A herd of deer are down by the sandy river shore for a drink of water. Under a tree, a peacock – its plumes spread open in the cool breeze – dances spiritedly one last time before dusk descends. At such a moment, Siddharth opened his eyes. His disciples observed that his body had become so weak that he couldn't walk. There was an *amla* tree bent over the water. Siddharth supported himself with one of its branches, stepped down into the river very slowly and rose again very painfully. He broke off a couple of *amla*s and was about to walk towards the forest when he fell down in a faint by the riverside. His disciples rushed to his side and carried him to the ashram. He recovered after a lot of care.

Koundinyo asked him, "Master, did you get to learn how sorrow ended?"

Siddharth shook his head and said, "No—not yet."

The remaining four disciples said, "Master, then sit in *yogasana* one more time and try to know whether suffering has an end."

Siddharth remained silent. As if to answer the disciples' question, a lunatic sang out from the interiors of the forests, playing on his *ektara*, "No it doesn't! It doesn't!"

Koundinyo asked," Is there no way of knowing, Lord?"

Siddharth answered, "I haven't found the Way yet. But see, this body has already become weak and useless from the rigour of excessive yoga. Now strength must be brought back to it. It is only then that the Way might again be searched for. No work is possible with a weak body and unenergised mind. Keep the body strong and vital, keep the mind vibrant and fresh. Be neither too luxurious, nor too dispassionate. Do not provide the body and mind with too much comfort, nor too much suffering. It will then remain vital and in working condition, and only then will it be able to walk in search of the Way. The strings of the *ektara* snap if pulled too hard. Likewise, the body and mind collapse from too much strain. Again, if the strings are allowed to loosen up too much, they do not make any music either. Likewise, if the body and mind are allowed to relax beyond bounds through too much pleasure and laziness, they become slothful and incapable of working. It is useless to lose energy through too much hard discipline. It is also futile to make it lazy through too much inactivity and pleasure. It is best to follow the middle path."

«««»»

From that day the disciples observed that Siddharth had given up smearing ash and sitting in rigorous yogic postures. Having abandoned the *nyash*, *kumbhak* (the holy pot), *tarpan* (ritual bathing while chanting mantras), *jap* (counting beads while meditating), *dhuni* and *dhunuchi* (essential ingredients of traditional *tapasya*), he spent his days begging from village to village, as he had done before. When he received a new garment, he wore it. When he received a good meal, he ate it. His disciples did not like this.

They believed that in order to be a Yogi, one had to light a fire around himself on hot days, and to immerse

Siddharth following the Middle Path, restoring strength to his body, his disciples leaving

himself in water throughout day and night when it was cold. One had to stand with arms upraised to the sky at certain times, or with bowed head, secure one's legs to the branches of trees at other times. Maybe have a *kul* berry the first day, a single bel leaf the second day, gradually only a drop of water, and then even give that up. Without such rigour, they believed, no results could be attained. So one night they left Siddharth alone and went away towards Kashi's Rishipattan—in search of a greater holiness.

The spot in the Urayil forests where the disciples had abandoned Siddharth was very quiet and lonely. Sal forests cast deep shadows across it all day and night. Human beings did not venture here too much. A deer or two, and sometimes a couple of squirrels scampered over the dry sal leaves, making a rustling noise.

Along this unresponsive lonely forest, the way to the village winded up to the banks of the Anjana river. There was a mighty banyan tree beside the river. Nobody knew how old it was. Its thick-knotted roots, climbing along the high banks like pythons, hung directly over the water. The base of the tree was beautifully framed with black stones. People offered prayers to the tree, believing some deity inhabited it. Women from the village on the other side of the river crossed over in very early mornings, with beautiful offerings of flowers and fruits. They sometimes thought they had caught a glimpse of a saffron-clad figure sitting underneath the tree. But the figure vanished into the darkness as soon as it saw them! On some days the woodcutters, returning after chopping wood in the forest, caught sight of a godlike male figure dressed in golden garments, sitting under the tree lighting it up. People believed there must be some god living there. Nobody had ever seen the god clearly, except for Punna.

A day after her marriage, the village headman's daughter Sujata had found Punna under the banyan tree, when she had gone there to offer prayers. She had brought her home. From that time Punna has been brought up in the headman's house like a daughter. Now she was ten years old. Sujata had no children of her own, and she had raised Punna like a daughter. She had sworn to the Banyan-tree Deity that if she had a son, she would light a ghee-fuelled lamp daily under his tree for one whole year and offer a special puja on the full moon of new year's day. Sujata's God had given her a priceless and precious son of her own, so Punna came to the banyan-tree every evening to light a ghee-fuelled lamp.

She has been coming for the past one year, but had never seen the god of the banyan tree clearly. Sometimes, even before she reached, the figure of the god would seem to become indistinct and fade like a shadow; sometimes while crossing the river back to the village alone on foot after leaving the lighted lamp under the tree, she would see the deity come and sit down on the stone seat!

But in the last few wintry months, Punna has been seeing the god daily, like a shadow through a thin mist! She had told this to nobody else but Sujata. Sujata had instructed her to take two fruits for the god every day, tied up in the corner of her sari. She had also told Punna that if any day the god revealed himelf to her clearly, or spoke to her, to tell him—"God! Keep my Sujata-ma, my father, my little brother and my grandfather the village headman safe and well! When I grow up, I pray that I may get a wonderful husband!"

And so Sujata started sending two fruits everyday through Punna to the god under the banyan tree. She didn't know, neither did Punna, that Siddharth came and sat on the cool stone seat every evening.

«««»»

It is year-end today; and tomorrow the full-moon of new year's day. Early in the morning Punna has left a beautifully decorated plate bearing five lamps and five fruits under the banyan—one each from her, her brother, her mother, her father and one from her grandfather the village-headman. The golden glow of late-afternoon sunlight bends to touch the foot of the tree. River Anjana flows steadily, extending the mark of its waters over the sunburnt sandy shores. On the other bank, paddy fields stretch till a long way off, interspersed by little villages surrounded by mango and jackfruit plantations. Earthen huts, roofs of straw, and a hill—the distance is visible like a cloud. Just by the riverside the dirt track runs through the fields, straight and narrow like the white border of a green sari. The daughters of the farmers walk along that road, carrying bundles of grass on their heads. They wear crimson saris and silver bangles on their wrists. A boy of tender years sleeps peacefully inside a bag they carry over their backs, his fists curled up. A little gust of cool wind from the river touches the face. A kite comes circling down from high above and slowly alights inside a thicket.

Punna watches as the day comes to an end. A herd of black buffaloes return over the sands. The milkman's son sits astride one of them, holding the long branch of a tree as a stick. Every evening he gives Punna a ride back to the village-headman's home atop his buffalo. He comes for the same reason today, calling from a long distance, "Hey-y…Punna-a." The boy's name is Swasti. On hearing his call, Punna quickly lights the five lamps and walks towards the direction of his voice.

«««»»

The *chaturdashi* moon rises in the east like a gold plate. Punna and Swasti travel on buffalo-back over the sandy shores. On the raised bank of the river, the base of the banyan tree glitters with the light of Punna's lamps. In that light, Punna and Swasti both clearly see the saffron-robed god sitting under the tree on the stone seat.

Swasti leaves after dropping Punna off on her doorstep. Sujata, after tying up the cows and calves and putting her little son to sleep, is arranging the vessels for the morning puja, when Punna comes in and says—"Mother, I saw the god today, for real, both Swasti and I. If you go there very early tomorrow morning, you will also see him. But I forgot to ask anything from him."

"If you had remembered, what would you have asked for, Punna?"asks Sujata. "That you and Swasti get married—am I right?"

But by then Punna has fled. When Sujata comes in after arranging everything for puja, she is already asleep beside her little brother.

Sujata's eyes remain sleepless that night. She calls Punna when it is still night. Punna opens the door to the cow-pen. In the light of a single lamp in the corner, she milks the cows. The cows feel a little cold in the chilly air of dawn. They are also a little afraid and confused and look here and there restlessly. Who has come to milk them so late in the night? But when Punna strokes their backs with her left hand and calls them by their names, they relax and stand still.

Sujata lights a stove at one side of the courtyard and goes to take a bath with water from the well. Punna finishes collecting the little milk, pours it inside a clean vessel and puts it on the stove. The milk begins to boil vigorously. Sujata comes back dressed in fresh clothes and tells Punna, "Go pick some flowers while I stir the milk."

There is a garden just beside the village-headman's house; it has plenty of marigold flowers. Punna weaves a garland with the flowers. She smears oil and sindoor on a few banyan-leaves and arranges them on the puja plate. She calls out to Sujata—"Ma, come, if we're any later than this, it'll be morning and you will miss the god."

Sujata pours the freshly boiled and thickened milk inside a new earthen cup and hands it to Punna, saying—"You go ahead with this, I'll follow with the plate of puja offerings and Manua." Manua is Sujata's son.

The village path is visible in parts in the darkness of dawn. Punna walks ahead with the cup of milk, raising a tinkling sound with her anklets. Sujata follows behind with her son, holding the plate in her right hand. She feels a little scared walking alone with Punna. When they are near Swasti's house, she says, "Why don't you call Swasti as well?"

Swasti doesn't need to be called. Hearing the sound of Punna's footsteps, he comes out at once bearing a stick and a light. The three walk through the fields. There is still a while left for night to end. Stars are still visible overhead. The fresh early morning air releases the clinging layer of overnight cowdung fume that hung low above the village like a white canopy and now floats up to the sky. A couple of partridges in the *ulu* thickets, and a few common mynahs in the *bakul* tree have already begun to chirp a little. A wagtail flies whistling across the field. The babblers alight with rustles and chirrups under the jackfruit tree. Swasti puts out the light and reaches the side of the river, bringing Sujata and Punna with him. The outlines of the trees in the distance have become more distinct. Standing on the riverside, Sujata sees a figure under the banyan tree. The glow from his saffron robe has tinged half of the sky above with the light of morning.

«««»»

Sujata and Punna offer puja to their hearts' content and leave with Siddharth's blessings. Swasti, unable to give him anything; wove a mat of *kushi* grass with a lot of

care, sitting alone by the riverside all day, and finally cooled it in river water. Siddharth hadn't come to the banyan tree yet. Swasti spreads the *kushi* mat on the stone seat, bows to Siddharth in his heart and walks away to the riverbank.

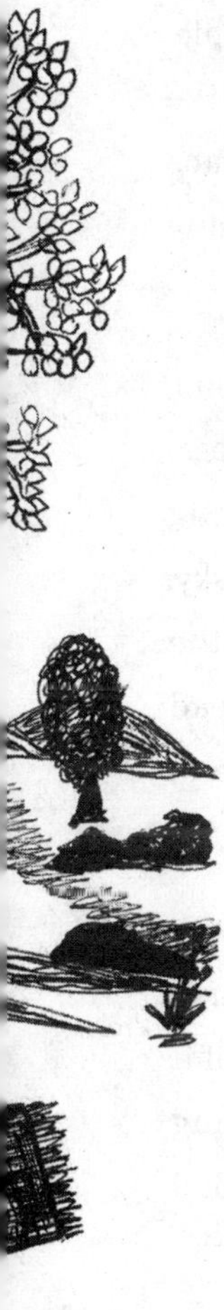

It was nearly evening. After bathing in the Anjana, Siddharth came and sat on the mat given by Swasti. The sweetly fragrant *kushi* mat washed in water soothes his mind. It seemed as if he could see up to the end of the world today, distinctly, clearly, in the light of the full moon.

Sitting on the *kushasana* over the stone seat that day, Siddharth resolves, Let the body survive or perish as it wills, I *will* see the End of Sorrow today. Without attaining Siddhi without becoming Buddha (Enlightened), I will not leave this seat. Sitting in *vajrasana*, Siddharth resolved –

"Ihashaney shushyutu me sharirong
Twagasthimangshang pralayaancha yatu

◀ *Sujata, Punna and Swasti offer puja to Buddha under the banyan tree*

Aprapya bodhing bahukalpadurlabhang

Naibashanath kaematashchalishyate."

At that instant, Maar, feared by the whole of existence, the one responsible for giving evil counsel to people, making them say harsh words and do bad deeds—the throne of that Maar began to shake violently. His face became crimson with rage, and Maar came rushing towards Buddha, roaring his battle cry.

The cronies of Maar also awakened in all directions, and came running – all of sin, sorrow, sooty blackness, ill repute, burning pain, dirt and dust – scattering themselves in all directions through land, water and sky. Maar drew a dark curtain over the full moon, and the moon stared out of its black veil like a red eye! Instead of light, the moon started to rain blood. Blood-spattered, the stars started guttering!

Crushing the sky inside one fist, and the underworld with one foot, Maar in his full glory stood facing Sidddharth today. His red shawl billowed in the wind, looking as if it has been dyed with human blood! A sword of lightning hung at his waist, a huge blood-gem was suspended from his crown, gold earrings hung from his ears; the fire-garland blazing on his breast was hung on thread spun of fire.

"Your *tapasya* for attaining Buddhattwa is all in vain!" Maar boastfully told Siddharth. "*Uttishtho*—get up from your seat! *Kameshwarohashmi*—I am Maar! No one in the three worlds can defeat me. *Uttishtho! Mahyabishayashthang bachang kurushwa*—rise and leave, do not attempt to gain victory over me. Obey me, and I will give you treasure comparable to the wealth of Indra, the king of heaven himself. Become the king of earth and rule amidst pleasure. What use is it ravaging your body with *tapasya*? No one can gain victory over me and attain Buddhattwa."

"Oh Maar!" said Siddharth. "I have been persevering to become Buddha (the Enlightened One) and engaging in *tapasya* through several lifetimes. This time I'll leave the seat only when I become enlightened. This is my pledge, whether the body remains or perishes—

Ihashaney shushyutu me sharirong
Twagasthimangshang pralayaancha yatu
Aprapya bodhing bahukalpadurlabhang
Naibashanath kaematashchalishyate.

Siddharth, Maar and Maari

Thrice Maar said, "*Uttishtho*, go away, leave *tapasya*!"

Thrice Buddha answered," No. No. No. *Naibashanath kaematashchalishyate*."

«««»»

Maar gave a blood-curdling roar and pulled down the sky, his eyes bloodshot with terrible rage. The blue sky with its moon and stars was ripped apart by his sharp nails and fell down, scattering into a hundred fragments like a midnight blue star spangled *neelambari* sari. There was no moon, no stars overhead; only the great nothingness, great darkness! It was as if something was rushing to engulf the earth with open jaws, dripping black saliva down its black tongue like thick blood! The instant Maar looked at this black visage, two rows of white teeth flashed out of the blue like lightning and ferociously ground against each other. From the interiors of that all-consuming open-jawed mouth, the followers of Maar rushed out with a terrible cry! The sun and the moon spun in their hands like two fiery wheels! Borne on a whirlwind, triumphantly blowing flags of dust, Maar and his followers whirled down, darkening the ten directions! They rain comets from the emptiness above like brooms of fire! They uproot trees from the earth, wrench up mountains, and hurl them like a furious unceasing hailstorm. It was as if thousands of mad horses belonging to Maar's battle troops were stamping about Buddhadev. Their hooves sparked lightning; burning blood foams out of their mouths and scatter around Buddha's banyan tree and his stone seat. Every tree, leaf and flower, every blade of grass in the Urayil forests burned today; the waters of the Anjana flow in whirlpools of burning blood and fire. Sharpening their swords on the edge of lightning and carrying burning torches, troops of blood germ emerge out of the darkness and fall in swarms over Buddhadev. The sky melts from their fiery breath, the wind burns, and the earth, like a fragment of smouldering ember, sparks fiery spray as it rotates in the whirlwind. In the midst of all this, Maar spins a blazing palm tree and cries—"Strike! Strike hard!"

In the meantime, responding to Maar's cry, Mahamari (Great Slayer) wakes up, ripping the underworld with his toenails. He gathers up all the dense black from the kohl-darkness of the deepest underworld, wraps it around himself like a blanket, and advances in a rush, shrieking at a terrible piercing pitch. The darkness billows all around him, and his dust-covered blanched hair blows in the wind, like a smoking comet filling up the sky. Heart-wrenching sobs are heard from all directions, and the three worlds are trembling from head to foot! As soon as the wind from Mahamari's body touches them, mountains and stones are reduced to dust, woods and glens start burning, rivers and oceans dry up. Nothing is visible anywhere, everything becomes a desert. Things fall down, collapse, burn, are charred and ground to dust and flow away as ash. Maari's shriek, Maar's roar and the terrible stench of burning flesh of the cremation grounds fill the three worlds.

It is the first watch of the night. The followers of Maar and those of Maari move about like fire-vomitting foxes, like bats with blood-red eyes, spewing fire from their mouths, crying out with blood-curdling sounds. The sky spins overhead; the earth spins underfoot, with a grating sound. They are like two hugo grinding stones trying to crush Buddhadev. Maar, carrying a lightning-torch in each hand, calls out to Buddha—"Flee, while there is still time. Stop your *tapasya*. I am warning you."

Buddhadev does not even look at Maar, nor listens to a single word he has to say. Maar's daughter Kaamna

(Desire) along with her two younger sisters Chhala and Kala try hard to break Buddha's mindfulness, sometimes by taking on the appearance of Goutami Ma, sometimes posing as Yasodhara, weeping and imploring pitifully with folded palms. To melt his heart and distract his concentration, they sometimes dance and sing seductively like Bidyadhari of the heavens, but are unable to lure him! He sits resolved in *bajrasana* today. Who is there who can break his meditation?

The fire of Maar makes heaven-earth-underworld trio tremble. Under his feet lie Indra-Chandra-Vayu-Varun, water, land and sky. Buddha's might has shattered his boastful pride today! Maar has failed to harm a single hair on Buddhadev's head. He has failed to dislodge a single leaf of Buddha's indestructible banyan tree, a single corner of the stone seat! How will Maar stand facing the Buddha even for a moment? He lacks the guts to even look at Buddhadev! Extinguishing his burning torches, Maar slowly creeps away from battle and flees to the deepest depths of Hell, to the territory of great darkness, blackening all the directions. Buddhadev sits alone and unafraid in the heart of the kohl-black darkness, mindfully meditating, hour after hour of the night.

«««»»

Night draws to an end. The earth still sporadically trembles at intervals in terror of Maar. The moon is not able to rise; morning does not dare arrive yet. At this point, having vanquished Maar and expelled Fear from all existence, Buddha rises finishing his meditation. He has attained the state of 'Buddha' today, after having found the end of sorrow. Holding up his right hand, he vows to protect the world, and reassures the gods in heaven with his left hand. A seven-hued light emanates from around his golden body. In this light, the universe has awakened with joyful celebration, having received life anew, adorning themselves anew. The Nairanjan river flows under Buddha's feet, sprinkling the waters of peace from bank to bank.

At Kashi, the Ganga river twists on its course like a sharp edged scimitar. Just below Rishipattan, the banks of the River Baruna were as hard as a mountain rock. In the caves and crevices along its sides reside the fake *brahmacharis*, with their knotted hair and ash-smeared bodies, lighting *dhunis*. Just above the bank was the Sarnath temple.

The temple grounds gave way to tree-shaded forests. There the real hermits resided. Deer did not feel afraid in their presence and flee, birds did not fly away from them. They hurt no one. Before anyone woke up in the morning, they came out of the forest once and took a bath in the river. They did not emerge from their forest retreat at any other time of the day or night. Debal Rishi had been staying in this place for the last few months along with Nalak, underneath a banyan tree.

It was the month of Asharh, the first month of the monsoon season. Strangely enough, the day refused to end, daylight refused to melt away. The sound of conch shells could be heard from the Sarnath temple, but the golden light of early dusk still glittered on the tree tops. Deer still grazed, little green birds chirruped and played about in the lingering patches of sunlight. Nalak sat alone and gazed quietly at the full-bodied rain-fed river of monsoon. He saw a white heron constantly flitting to and fro between the two banks of the river, as if unable to make up its mind about which bank it should choose to build its nest.

The unceasing flow of the river in this rainy season tugs at Nalak's heartstrings all day today, reminding him of the *vardhan* forest, of their little village. His heart ran to his mother in the earthen hut in the shade of the tamarind tree, and rushed back again. He wanted to go to his mother, but did not want to leave the Rishi alone. Like the heron, he was restless and undecided, forever making journeys to and fro!

Debal Rishi gave Nalak permission to visit his mother. But Nalak had also heard him mention that Buddhadev was approaching Rishipattan. So many years had passed since Nalak had left home; he hadn't seen his mother in ages! Still, he was not able to give up this little longing of seeing Buddhadev.

He sat all alone on the riverbank and debated whether to go or not. So many boats had come and gone since morning, ferrying so many people to their respective homelands. So many ferrymen had called out to Nalak, "Will you come?"

It was evening. The single remaining ferry, its sail up, came towards Nalak from far away. Its light was visible. The small light glistened as it floated across the river. There would be no boat to come this way, after this one left. Nalak mentally prayed to Debal Rishi—"Please grant that I am able to set my eyes on Buddhadev."

«««»»

Gradually the ferry arrives and touches the wharf beside the forest retreat. Nalak sails home to see his mother. He hasn't seen her in so many years. And at that very instant, Buddhadev crosses the bank of the Baruna river and alights at the Sarnath retreat. Oh, if only Nalak had stayed behind another day!

«««»»

The boat carrying Nalak travels through many lands, stopping at ever so many crowded wharfs and shores, dropping off each person at his village. As the older travellers get down at their stations, new ones board the ferry and fill up their places. Nalak's boat sometimes speeds with full sail, cutting through the water like an arrow in the morning wind; at other times it travels in the dark of night, so slowly that it doesn't appear to move at all, marking the black waters with the mellow reflection of the flame of a single lamp. In the rainy season, the river fills up with water. Previously only the high riverbanks had been visible. Now the fields above, the trees and huts in the villages across, even the temples in the distance can be seen. The water increases its depth and submerges all the sandy shores.

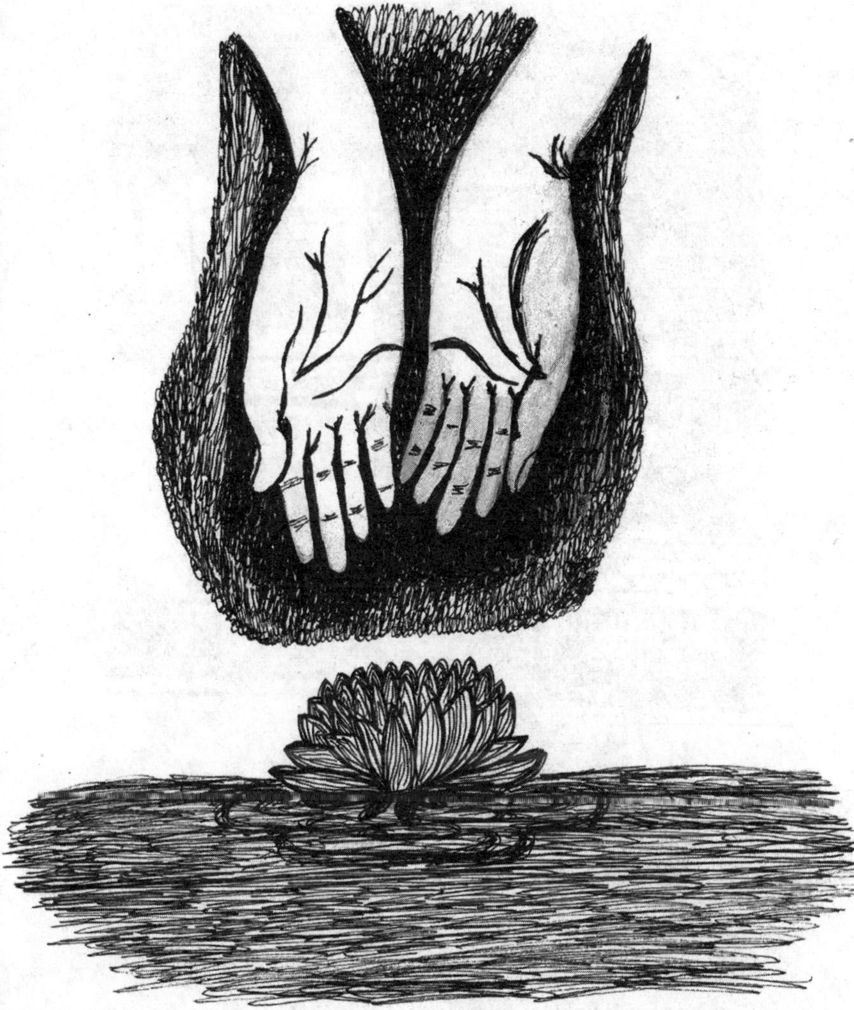

Nalak floats a flower in the river

Nalak returning home. A beggar singing in his courtyard

It is the month of Sravan when the boat drops Nalak off at his home station. Rain splashes down, drowning the bases of the bamboo sticks planted by the riverside. Water dances about everywhere! The fields, small water bodies and ploughed lands are full to the brim; the steps of the river wharf are under water, below the flow of current, immersed in the fresh waters of the monsoon.

Nalak stands on the riverbank and looks at a flower somebody has floated. It has travelled all the distance over the water and has touched the edge of the wharf. He watches the waves pull it towards the bank, then push it away towards the water, and again tug it back. Nalak picks up the flower from the water and, saying a prayer in Buddhadev's name, again floats it in mid-river. Then he walks slowly away towards his home, the rain soaking him to the skin.

Long ago, so long back that he cannot remember, Nalak had left home with the Rishi, just like this flower. He had left his mother and floated away from homebound existence. After a long time, he has floated back home, just like the flower, and lodged himself near his mother's lap. Would Buddhadev ever come to this land? Would he pick up this lodged flower, and set it free to float again in the Ganga of joy?

Nalak can see his home now. He can see his mother sitting in the courtyard. A beggar is standing at the centre of the yard and singing–

Dressing Him up as a beggar!
O what playfulness is this...

GLOSSARY

Abir: Coloured powder people smear on each other's faces and bodies in a spirit of play and brotherhood during the Indian summer festival of colours, 'Holi'.

Agamani: Songs of devotion and joy that herald Goddess Durga's descent onto earth to her parents' home once every year in the autumnal months, from her snowy abode in Mount Kailash where she lives with her husband and their children.

Amla: Indian gooseberry, *Phyllanthus emblica*.

Asana/Yogasana: A series of bodily poses recommended in Yoga, first popularly synthesised and detailed by the ancient sage Patanjali in his Yoga sutras. Asanas when practised correctly have the potential not only to ensure agility and suppleness of the body, but also to powerfully unite the mind, body and spirit.

Asharh: The first month of the monsoon season.

Ashwattha: The sacred fig tree, or *Ficus religiosa*, also known as peepul. This is the tree under which Gautama Buddha is said to have achieved enlightenment.

Atal: The first of the seven underworlds.

Bakul: The *Mimusops elengi*, a sacred flowering plant. All its parts including bark, leaves, roots and resin are used in traditional medicine and/or have ceremonial significance.

The flowers of the bakul, white and beautifully fragrant, are often found growing profusely at temple entrances and are used in romantic invocations.

Brahmachari: One who observes celibacy. The first phase of life, according to the Hindu belief, where one focuses on learning and developing oneself as a student and refrains from the sexual act.

Buddhatwa: Buddhahood that is, the state of being Buddha, or enlightened.

Chaturdashi: The fourteenth day of the *shukla paksha* (the fifteen day period from New Moon to Full Moon) or the *krishna paksha* (the fifteen day period from Full Moon to New Moon). It is a day of great religious significance, coming once every fortnight as explained above.

Chhala: Bark of trees or the skin.

Dhuni: A sacred altar in the ground, where a flame is kindled and offerings made to the fire, often accompanied by sacred chants. The altar is symbolic of the female *yoni*, or vagina, and thus represents the creative feminine principle of the universe, or Shakti, from where everything in the universe manifests and takes birth. Sitting beside or worshipping at the *dhuni* is believed to purify and balance the energies within.

Dhunuchi: Traditional resin-burner, usually earthen, with a long stem and an expanded cavity on top, used during religious worship to offer homage to the gods. Usually burning coal is placed inside in conjunction with coconut husk and a sprinkling of resin, and this emits a strong, somewhat suffocating odour that is said to drive away impurities and pests like mosquitoes from the atmosphere.

Durba: A type of sacred grass with three blades, used ritually with flowers to worship deities. It is also used by elders to convey blessings and prayers for well-being during social ceremonies like marriages or baby showers.

Dwitiya: The second day of either the full moon or the new moon. In the current context, it refers to the crescent moon appearing during the second day of the *shukla paksha*, and is compared to the shape of an elephant tusk.

Ektara: A one-stringed musical instrument popular with wandering minstrels and bards, played by plucking with one finger.

Ghee: Clarified butter made from the milk of a buffalo or cow, used in South Asian cooking.

Hom puja: Burning a sacred fire as an offering to the gods. Ghee and other materials are usually fed to this fire and it is believed to purge and purify.

Jaam: A dark purple berry with a sweet-pungent flavour and a hard seed inside. Widely found, sold and eaten all over India, especially in the months of late summer and monsoon. Hindi-*jamun*.

Jap: The act of chanting a prayer or the name of a deity repeatedly, keeping count on a sacred string of beads called a mala.

Kaash: A kind of grass native to the Indian subcontinent, growing up to three metres in height, with soft and slender white flowers that bloom during the autumnal months. *Kaash* flowers are nostalgically associated by Bengalis with the advent of their biggest festival, Durga Puja.

Kala: The personification of Time itself, with its associations of eternity, mortality, and inevitability. Also, one of the names of the god of death, Yama, and the god of destruction, Shiva.

Kubo: Crow pheasant, also called the coucal, this bird belongs to the cuckoo family and inhabits semi-rural sparsely habited regions, gardens and lightly wooded forests. They are known for their characteristic '*kub kub*' call. All of them belong in the subfamily *Centropodinae* and the *genus Centropus*. The great, or common coucal (*C. sinensis*), called crow pheasant in India, is 48 to 56 cm (19 to 22 inches) long. It is black with brown mantle and wings. Its range is from India to southern China and Malaysia.

Kumbhak: In yoga and pranayama, the pause between an inhale and an exhale. A complete breath cycle is thought to be one where every inhale and exhale is followed by a *kumbhak*.

Kushasana: A small mat made of *kush* grass, often used for meditation.

Kushi: A vessel used in worship, usually made of copper and resembling a spoon.

Maar: In Buddhist legend, Maar is a demon who put obstacles in Siddharth's path to enlightenment by sending him his daughters in the form of beautiful and seductive women. Apart from being a personification of forces that prevent one from attaining enlightenment, Maar is also associated with violence, death and desire.

Mahabuddha: The nature of being perfectly endowed with the highest enlightenment that characterises the Buddha.

Nahabatkhana: A music tower of sorts where, during important religious or social ceremonies, people sit in the upper storey and play music as in a concert.

Neelambari: Blue as the sky, often referring to a woman's garment or sari.

Nyash: Yogic exercise of breath control and/or touching different parts of the body accompanied by sacred chants in order to evoke certain spiritual states. Note that *kumbhak*, which appears alongside *nyaash* in the text, also means ‹retention of breath; religious or yogic exercise.

Papia: Hawk cuckoo or brain fever bird.

Parijat: Considered to be a divine tree, the *parijat* (*shefali/ shiuli* in Bengali and *harshringar* in Hindi) bears the botanical name of *Nycatanthes arbortristis* and is native to

South Asia and Southeast Asia. It is a shrub with flaky grey bark. This 'night flowering' tree has tales of its romantic origin. A certain princess Parijataka was in love with the sun and when spurned, she committed suicide. A flowering tree sprung from her ashes. Unable to bear the sight of the lover, the tree flowers only at night and sheds the pretty white flowers with a bright orange centre, at dawn, like tear drops, forming a carpet of snow-white petals at the feet of the tree and its bare branches, an enchanting but also a somewhat sad sight. Hence the name, 'tree of sorrow'.

Rasatal: The infernal world. One of the levels of the underworld believed to be comprised of seven different levels.

Sal: The Sal tree (*Shorea robusta*) is indigenous to India and occurs mainly in the northern and central Indian regions. The plant belongs to the *Dipterocarpaceae* botanical family.

Shiuli: The *Nyctanthes arbortristis*, also known as *parijat*. It has small white flowers with a distinct orangish-red centre often used for dying clothes orange. They have four to eight petals arranged above a vibrant orange tube in a pinwheel pattern. These highly fragrant *parijat* flowers bloom at night and fills the air with a beautiful fragrance that lingers even after these flowers drop to the ground.

Siddha: A master, someone who has achieved perfection on the physical as well as the spiritual plane. Siddhas may possess metaphysical or occult capabilities as well.

Siddhi: The attainment of enlightenment.

Suktara: Sirius or Suktara, also known as the Dog Star or Sirius A, is the brightest star in the Earth's night sky. The name means 'glowing' in Greek. Since Sirius is so bright, it was well-known to the ancients.

Sutal: The foundational level of the underworld believed to be comprised of seven different levels.

Tarpan: The ritual of offering water to ancestors or deities as an act of grateful remembrance or appeasement.

Tapasya: The act of practicing deep immersive meditation and rigour for long stretches of time towards a spiritual goal.

Tintiri: The tamarind tree, the *Tamarindus indica*.

Ulu: A shrill sound made by women by touching their tongues to the roof of their palate and through pursed-up lips. It is considered auspicious and is ritually performed during important social and religious ceremonies.

Vajrasana: A kneeling posture practised in yoga, where one sits on one's heels with the knees and insteps touching the ground, and the first toe of either foot touching each other, while keeping the spine straight.

Yogasana: See 'asana' above.

Abanindranath Tagore (1871–1951) was an artist and writer from the illustrious Tagore family, and a nephew of Rabindranath Tagore. The principal innovator of the Bengal school of art, he created a distinctive Swadeshi style of art at a time when only western models were being imitated and practised in contemporary India. He revitalised Rajput and Mughal art into ethereal watercolours, and his later works incorporated Chinese and Japanese influences as well. He was appointed by Calcutta University as the Bageswari Professor of Oriental Art, and his writings and lectures on art remain relevant and important to art theory and practice to this day. His literary works, of delight to children and adults alike – *Buro Angla, Khirer Putul, Bhoot-Potrir Deshe, Nalak* and *Raj Kahini* – are marked by the delightful whimsy of his imagination and brought alive by his singular ability to paint pictures with words.

Urbi Bhaduri has been bewitched by the magic of words for as long as she can remember. She is grateful to stories for teaching her almost everything she knows of life today.

After completing her Masters in English from Jadavpur University, she has been exploring her strengths in different capacities—as a writer, editor and translator freelancing with publishing houses, newspapers and other organisations, and as a facilitator in the developmental sector, holding experiential workshops on poetry, memoir, self-discovery, deep listening, gender and entrepreneurship with young people who inhabit the urban margins, mostly in the streets and slums of Kolkata. She moves home frequently, and has lived all over India with her husband, her four dogs and more recently, with a baby girl.